W9-BMP-147

EAN

ISBN-13: 978-0-439-20772-0
ISBN-10: 0-439-20772-X

9 780439 207720

50499

S

THE SECRETS OF DROON

THE TOWER OF THE ELF KING

TONY ABBOTT

SCHOLASTIC

The Tower of
the Elf King *

A Magical World Awaits You
Read

THE SECRETS OF DROON

The Tower of
the Elf King

by Tony Abbott
Illustrated by David Merrell

SCHOLASTIC INC.
New York Toronto London Auckland Sydney
Mexico City New Delhi Hong Kong Buenos Aires

Book design by Dawn Adelman

ISBN-13: 978-0-439-20772-0
ISBN-10: 0-439-20772-X

27 26 25 24 23 22 21 20 19 18 17 16   7 8 9 10 11 12/0

Printed in the U.S.A.   40
First Scholastic printing, August 2000

To my parents,
for making a house where books ruled

Contents

One

Dream Pictures

"Hey, Eric! Watch me!"

Eric Hinkle looked up in time to see his friend Neal do a cannonball into his backyard pool.

Splash!

It was hot and sunny in Neal's backyard. His parents were having a big cookout. Everyone was laughing, swimming, and eating.

But Eric couldn't get into it. All he could

think about was a dream he'd had last night.

A dream about . . . Droon.

Ssss! Neal's mother set a pot of bubbling chili on the grill. Then she loaded on some hot dogs.

Droon was the magical world Eric and his friends Neal and Julie had discovered while cleaning up Eric's basement one day.

They'd found a small empty closet. As soon as they went inside — *whoosh!* — the floor vanished and a staircase appeared.

A staircase to the wonderful world of Droon.

Droon was a land of awesome adventure. A land of excitement.

And sometimes danger. But Eric loved it.

He, Julie, and Neal had made good friends in Droon. One was a princess named Keeah. Another was a wizard named Galen. Together, they were fighting a wicked sorcerer named Lord Sparr. The kids were helping them make sure Sparr didn't take over Droon.

After each visit, the kids couldn't wait to go back. Sometimes, when Keeah needed help, she sent a message through an enchanted soccer ball. Other times, the kids dreamed about Droon. That's how they knew when to return.

But this time, Eric wasn't so sure he wanted to return. He'd seen a face in his dream.

The face of something terrifying.

The first thing he did when he woke up was draw a picture of it.

Now he had to show the picture to his friends. But no one else could see. Droon was a secret.

"Hey, Neal!" Eric called out. "Where's Julie?"

"Coming soon!" Then Neal did a goofy dive and flopped into the water on his stomach.

Eric looked around. No one was watching, so he pulled out the picture and stared at it.

It stared right back.

With three angry red eyes.

"Not even Sparr has three eyes!" he mumbled.

"Chili dog?" asked a voice over his shoulder.

Eric quickly covered the paper. "No, thanks," he said. Then he looked up. "Julie!"

Julie was in a T-shirt and shorts. She sat down at the picnic table and began chomping on her hot dog. "Why aren't you in the pool?"

"I dreamed about Droon last night," Eric said. "But the only thing I remember is . . . this."

He showed Julie the drawing.

Julie nearly dropped her food. "Oh, my gosh! You made a drawing, too?"

She pulled a sheet of paper from her pocket and placed it on the table next to Eric's picture.

Eric blinked. "And I thought mine was scary!"

Julie's drawing showed a mouth with two rows of long teeth sticking out. But the teeth weren't the worst part. The worst part was the fire pouring out between them.

Neal came splashing over to the table, drying himself with a towel. "What's this, art class?"

"Scary art class," said Julie. "Take a look. Here's what we've been dreaming about."

"Whoa, a three-eyed monster eating my mom's extra-hot chili!" said Neal with a laugh.

"Yeah," whispered Eric. "All we need is a nose and we've got the creepiest monster ever!"

Neal stopped laughing. "You know what's weird? I dreamed about a nose last night."

Eric jumped up from the table. "Draw it right now. This is important. It could be a clue to what's happening in Droon!"

"I don't draw too well," said Neal. He looked around. "But the nose looked like . . . this!"

He took four chocolate chip cookies from the dessert plate and stacked them between the drawings. "That's the nose."

Eric frowned. "It looks like a pig nose."

"Exactly!" said Neal. "With three nostrils. It was huffing and puffing. It sneezed a lot, too."

"That's not very scary," said Julie.

"Did I mention the nose was drippy?" he added.

"That's it!" said Eric. "We need to go to Droon right now!" He stuffed the pictures in his pocket.

Neal snatched the cookies.

"Don't hog the food, son!" his father called.

"I'll share!" Neal said. Then he ran into the house to change. Two minutes later they were all at Eric's back door.

"You know what I think is cool?" asked Julie as they entered Eric's house.

"That we can spend all day in Droon and still be back in time for chili dogs?" said Neal.

"Besides that," said Julie. "It means we're a team. It took all of us together to figure out that there's some kind of monster in Droon."

"And that we need to go back," Eric added, charging through the kitchen and down to the basement. It was still pretty messy there. They never did finish cleaning it up.

Someday we'll get to it, Eric thought. Then he grinned. *But not today!*

They quickly pulled aside the cartons that blocked the little door under the basement stairs.

Neal opened the door. Inside was a small closet, completely bare except for a single light hanging from the ceiling. The three kids piled in.

"Ready to face the monster?" Eric asked.

Julie smiled. "Ready."

Click! Neal flicked off the light.

Whoosh! The floor below them vanished. They were standing on the top step of a long, glimmering staircase. The staircase to Droon.

As they started down, Eric recalled that Droon and his world — the Upper World — were connected by more than a magical staircase.

On their last adventure, Princess Keeah had come into Eric's basement for a minute. Then she said she had been there before!

Talk about secrets!

Galen had told them the staircase had been sealed for many years before the kids found it. So what did Keeah mean that she had been to the Upper World before? When? How? Why?

This time, Eric would ask her.

The stairs curved through a thin layer of pink clouds. The sky below was turning purple. It was the end of the day in Droon.

Neal peered down the stairs. "Hey! I

should have kept my trunks on, after all. There's a swimming pool down there —"

Suddenly, the stairs began to wobble.

"Uh-oh," said Julie. "Should we go back up?"

The stairs shivered and quivered.

"We can't!" Eric said. "Hurry, or we'll fall off."

They rushed down the steps two at a time.

"Prepare to dive!" said Neal.

Then Eric squinted over Neal's shoulder.

"Wait! That's not a swimming pool," he said.

"It's not?" said Neal, leaning forward.

Below them sat a giant cauldron, boiling fiercely. Red and blue flames licked up the sides.

"It's more like . . . a pot of chili!" cried Julie.

"I hope the cook isn't Lord Sparr!" Neal said.

Then — *whoosh!* — the stairs vanished.

The three friends fell through the air, straight toward the boiling pot.

"Help!" Eric screamed.

Hiss! Bubble! Splort! went the pot.

Two

The Ceremony of Truth

Zamm! A sudden blue light sizzled over the kids. They stopped falling. They stopped moving. They hung just inches above the hissing pot.

"Are we . . . cooked?" asked Neal.

"I don't think so," said Julie.

"This cauldron is on some kind of balcony," said Eric. "And it looks like there's a castle behind us —"

"My friends!" called a bright voice.

It was Princess Keeah. She ran across the stone balcony toward the kids. She was dressed in a blue tunic with a golden belt. A crown circled her head.

"You nearly became part of our spell!" she said. "I stopped you with only seconds to spare."

"Hey, I was just hoping we weren't the secret ingredient in Sparr's evil soup," Neal said.

A roar of laughter came from the castle. It was the warm voice of Galen Longbeard, first wizard of Droon. "It's not soup," he said. "It's not Sparr's. And it's certainly not to be eaten!"

Together with Keeah, Galen raised his hands and — *zzz!* — more blue light fell over the kids. They floated to the ground beside the pot.

Eric looked around. "We're in Jaffa City."

Keeah nodded. "This is the balcony outside my room. Galen and I are in the middle of an ancient spell called the Ceremony of Truth. We're using it to find out what happened to Sparr."

Eric glanced at his friends. "What do you mean?" he asked. "Is Sparr . . . missing?"

Keeah nodded slowly. "For nearly a whole moon no one has seen him. We're hoping that he won't bother us anymore. But we can't be sure until we find out where he is."

Eric remembered the last time he'd seen the wicked sorcerer. Sparr had been lying on the frozen lake near his evil fortress of Plud. He had been hurt.

But even in his pain, Sparr had stared up at Eric with eyes that said, *It is not over. Not over.*

Hsss! The cauldron began to hiss wildly.

Galen leaned over and sniffed the pot. "It is ready. Keeah, as part of your wizard training, would you do the honors?"

"Yes, sir!" she said brightly.

"Ready, Max?" Galen called over the side of the balcony to his assistant.

Max, an orange-haired spider troll, stood on the ground below. With his eight legs, he was holding up a large round board painted with brightly colored circles like a target.

"Ready, master!" he chirped.

At once, Keeah took a large ladle and thrust it into the boiling pot. When she lifted it out, it was thick with long white strands.

Julie nudged Eric. "That looks like spaghetti!"

Keeah went to the edge of the balcony and flung the goop off the ladle.

It fell through the air and — *splat!* — struck the target in the center.

"Direct hit!" Max chirped.

"Everyone, hurry!" said Keeah excitedly.

They all raced down to the courtyard.

Galen peered at the target. "Is he there?"

Julie asked, "Is *who* there?"

"Lord Sparr," Keeah said, leaning over. "Galen is looking for his face in the strands."

"There! A shape!" Max chirped. "I'd know those ear fins anywhere!"

Galen squinted at the blob. Then he sniffed it and walked completely around it. "Yes, it is Sparr," he said finally, poking the white stringy strands. "He is somewhere in the dark lands. But it's not clear what he is up to."

Neal nudged Eric. "A spaghetti Sparr? Makes me think of meatballs. . . ."

"Those are the Ninns!" Julie said with a laugh.

The Ninns were Sparr's plump, red-faced warriors. They were slow-witted and always angry.

"Is this actually *magic*?" Eric asked.

Galen laughed. "An ancient form of it, yes. You make a mess, but sometimes it works."

"If we learn that Sparr is gone, I'll happily clean up!" added Max as he pulled some white strands from his thick orange hair.

"Wow," said Julie. "What if it is true? If Sparr really is gone, wouldn't Droon be at peace?"

Galen smiled sadly. "So you would think. But the Ninns are leaving his dark lands in vast numbers. Something is up."

"Also, we've heard rumors about dangerous new creatures roaming Droon," said Keeah.

Eric looked at Julie and Neal. "New creatures? I almost forgot!" He pulled the drawings from his pocket and held them together. "Something like this?"

"How scary!" said Keeah.

"It has a nose, too," said Julie. "Neal, show them the cookies. We need the whole picture."

"The cookies?" Neal grinned. "Well, I, uh, sort of ate them. On the stairs. I was hungry!"

Julie narrowed her eyes at him. "Anyway, the monster had a pig nose."

"A pig nose . . ." Galen said. He gave the pictures, then the kids, a quizzical look. "I've never seen anything like it. Not in all of Droon."

"And that," Max chimed in, "is saying a

lot! My master Galen has seen nearly every beast —"

Blam! Blam! The giant gates of Jaffa City rocked. Someone was pounding on them.

"Help!" came a cry from outside the walls.

The palace guards opened the gates at once. Before them stood a small purple creature that looked a lot like a pillow.

"It's Khan!" said Max. "King of the Lumpies!"

Everyone ran over as Khan staggered in.

"M-my . . . village . . ." he stammered. "It's been robbed! By a fire-breathing monster! A monster with . . . three eyes!"

Three

The Plundered Village

Eric and Julie rushed to show Khan their drawings.

"It's him!" said the Lumpy king as he rested on the palace steps. "I saw the monster for only a moment. But those eyes! I'll never forget them!"

"Calm yourself, my dear Khan," Galen said.

"I can't be calm!" he replied. "Even my

beautiful crown was stolen. The legendary treasure of the Lumpies is gone. All the gold and jewels passed down from Lumpy to Lumpy since the beginnings of Droon. All of it, stolen in the dead of night."

The tassels on Khan's shoulders slumped as he spoke. Eric had never seen Khan so sad.

"We'll help you find your treasure," Eric said firmly. "I think it's why we're here. We dreamed of this monster. So we'll find him and get your treasure back. Right?"

Julie and Neal nodded.

"Galen?" said Keeah. "May I go, too?"

The wizard stroked his beard. "Yes, all of you should go. Keeah, take your magic harp. But be careful. We still don't know all of its powers."

"Yes, sir," she said.

Galen turned on his heels. "Max, get

the target. We'll try the Ceremony of Truth again. We will get to the bottom of this problem yet!"

As Galen and Max strode away, the princess called out, "Magic harp . . . come to me!"

Instantly, a dark shape flew out from her window high above them. It circled the balcony once, then landed gently in Keeah's arms.

"Awesome!" said Eric. "Now *that* is magic."

The instrument was called a bowharp. Shaped like a U, it bore two sets of strings crossing each other. It had once belonged to Keeah's mother, Queen Relna. But Keeah hadn't had it for long, and she still didn't know everything it could do.

"Galen told me that the harp was made by someone called the Maker," said Keeah as she slung it over her shoulder. "No one has seen him for years. But I'll show you one thing I discovered. Is everyone ready to go?"

Khan and the kids nodded.

"Then hold still," said Keeah. She spoke some strange words, then plucked the harp strings — *pling! blong!* Suddenly a rosy light beamed from the harp and fell over them all. The air quivered around the children.

"It feels like we're moving," said Julie.

"We are!" said Keeah. Then *plang!* — the song ended, the rosy light vanished, and they found themselves at the walls of a village surrounded by sand.

"Awesome!" said Neal. "Where are we now?"

"The deserts of Lumpland," said Keeah. "The scene of the crime. Where we might find clues to where the monster went next."

Khan led them into the village just as the sun vanished below the horizon and the first stars began twinkling in the sky.

The Lumpies' houses were made of dried mud and were stacked one on top of the other.

"The robbers came while we were sleeping," the king said. "They stole everything. Jewels, gold, silver. Even our kitchen utensils!"

"How greedy can a monster be?" asked Neal.

"Indeed," Khan went on. "Try cooking without pots and pans! Very messy business!"

They passed down one narrow street after another. Here and there were broken windows. Even the street lamps were dark.

"They stole your streetlights?" asked Julie.

"The silver lamps of my grandmother

once used to light our way," Khan said. "But not anymore!"

Finally, the king brought them to his own house. He called it his palace, but it wasn't much larger than the other Lumpies' homes.

Khan pointed to a hole in the front door. "Look, even my copper doorknob was taken!"

Inside, Khan showed them his sleeping chamber, then turned away.

"The sight of it makes me weak," he said.

A small stand next to the bed lay empty.

"I took off my crown last night and put it there, as I always do," Khan said. "Later, there was a noise and I awoke. It was dark, but I saw the monster. We tussled, but he took the crown. Then he and his helpers raced away."

"You're sure the Ninns didn't do this?" Eric asked. "Galen said they're popping up all over Droon."

Khan shook his head. "The Ninns have simple minds," he replied. "They need someone to lead them. Besides, no Ninn has three fiery eyes. This creature was different."

"Speaking of different," said Julie, "what's this?" From the floor she picked up a flat green object the size and shape of a coin.

"It looks like a scale from the monster's skin!" said Khan. He sniffed it. "Yes! I know the smell! Good work, Julie. We can use this scale to track him down!"

Without another word, Khan shot straight out of his house. The kids followed him.

A pale half moon had risen over the village. It cast a silvery light over the desert sand.

"How are we going to track the monster?" said Eric. "This desert is huge."

"You forget what made the Lumpies famous!" Khan said. With a wink he sniffed the small green scale, then pushed his nose into the air. *Sniff! Sniff!*

"The scent is faint, but still there," Khan said, squinting out over the dunes. Then he pointed. "That way. We must follow!"

Ten minutes later, the small troop set out.

Khan took the lead. He stopped every now and then to sniff the scale, then picked up the trail again.

After nearly an hour of trudging across the moonlit sands, they stopped to rest behind a huge sand dune.

While Khan passed a canteen to Julie and Neal, Keeah practiced softly on her harp.

"I think I'll try to see what's out there," Eric said. He stepped away from the camp.

"We'll start soon," said Keeah. "Don't go far."

"Okay," he said. Then he stopped. "Keeah?"

She looked up from her harp. "Yes?"

"Well . . . you said you were in the Upper World before. Was that true? I mean, how?"

The princess shrugged her shoulders slightly. "It's a mystery," she said. "When I saw the trees outside your basement, I just knew I had been there before. I don't know how. I don't know when. But my father says it's impossible."

Eric took a deep breath. "Maybe your mother knows. I mean, you found her magic harp. Maybe it means you'll find her soon, too."

Keeah smiled. "I hope I will."

Keeah's mother, Queen Relna, was under a spell. First she had been a falcon, then a dragon. But where she was now and what form she was in, no one knew.

Eric left Keeah and climbed alone to the top of the dune. Looking up, he saw billions of bright stars twinkling in every direction.

Then something twinkled down below, too.

Eric lowered his gaze. "Holy crow!" he gasped.

At the bottom of the dune was a fire.

No . . . many fires. And tents. Hundreds of tents, spreading far into the distance.

An army of tents. Red ones.

"Ninns!" he hissed. "I've got to warn the others!" But as he turned to rush back, the ridge at the top of the dune gave way. He hit the sand and began to roll.

The more he tried to stop himself, the faster he rolled. Over and over he went, faster and faster, until — *whoosh!*

He crashed right through the back of one of the tents and stopped with a thud.

Yellow light flooded over him.

Eric squinted. Then he stared.

Right into the face of a fierce red Ninn!

Four

In the Company of Ninns

Eric gaped at the face before him.

It was a Ninn, all right.

The chubby red cheeks. The sharp chin. The pointed ears that stuck out to the side. The deep-set black eyes the size of marbles.

But this one was different from any other Ninn Eric had ever seen.

This one was wearing a dress!

"What you?" grunted the Ninn, leaning over, nose to nose with Eric.

"Uh . . . I'm Eric?" he answered.

"Humph!" the Ninn grunted. She pulled away and sat down on a rug that lay like a floor over the sand. Before her, a small pot sizzled over a fire. Smoke from the fire wafted up through a hole in the ceiling of the tent.

Eric wondered if he should bolt out of there as soon as possible. But what if she screamed? What if Sparr was right outside? He looked around.

The inside of the tent was lined with sacks and bundles. So it was true, Eric thought. The Ninns *had* been traveling.

Maybe he could find out where.

"Wahh!" came a squeaky sound from behind the Ninn. Eric nearly jumped out of his skin.

A small Ninn, a child of maybe two or three, sat playing quietly behind the woman.

The child already wore the fierce expression of all Ninn warriors.

The Ninn woman scooped a small brown ball from the pot she was stirring. She held it out to the child, who grunted softly, then ate it.

Eric turned to the Ninn. "Is Sparr near here?"

She cast her eyes at the fire under the pot. "Sparr," she grunted. "Sparr . . . gone."

The words sent a shock through him.

"Gone? Sparr *gone*?" he repeated. "Where?"

The Ninn grumbled under her breath as she spooned more food onto a plate.

"Secret place," she said. "No one knows."

"Is he . . . dead?" Eric asked.

"Not dead. Not alive. Now we follow Gryndal."

"Gryndal?" Eric repeated. "Who is he?"

"He worse," the Ninn said. "Lizard. Monster. Gryndal use Ninns to help him build tower."

Eric guessed that the monster was the same one they'd been tracking.

"Gryndal is building a tower?" asked Eric. "Where is it? And what is it for?"

The Ninn grumbled and shrugged her massive shoulders. "Sparr gone. Gryndal worse. Ninns not happy."

For a moment, the only sound was the crackling of the fire. Then there was a grunt from outside. A loud grunt. The tent flap jostled.

"Oh, no!" Eric gasped. "I better go —"

"Be still!" the Ninn woman said. In a flash, she flung a thick blanket over him.

Eric didn't move. He didn't breathe.

Through a small hole in the blanket Eric saw a giant Ninn warrior barrel into the tent as if he lived there.

Then Eric realized . . . he probably did.

The small Ninn yipped once and the warrior patted its fuzzy head. Then the Ninn turned to the woman and growled and grunted strange words. She answered him back the same way.

It was probably the Ninn language, Eric thought. It sounded very strange. Like gargling.

Whatever she said, the warrior didn't seem to like it. He began stomping around the tent, banging things and slapping his hands together.

"Me hungry! Me food . . . now!"

He stared at her, angry and mean-looking.

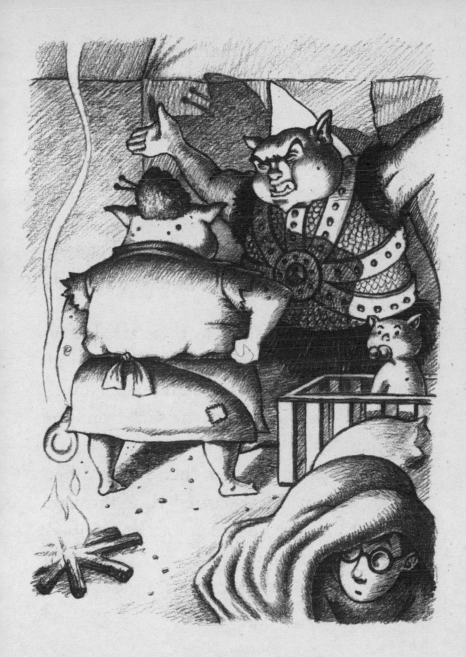

Suddenly, the woman yelled, "Thalak!"

The warrior bolted upright. He staggered back, his beady eyes squinting at the woman. He grumbled loudly, then — *swoosh!* — the tent flap went up and he was gone.

"Whoa!" whispered Eric. "Saved!"

The woman whipped off the blanket. "Go," she said. "Yak-yak! Far from here. And take."

She held out a small leather sack. Into it she plopped a large helping of the food she'd been cooking on the fire. "Go. Now!"

Wide-eyed, Eric took the sack from the woman. "Thank you. You're very nice."

The woman nodded, then swished her hands at him. Eric scurried back through the tent the way he had come. He climbed back up the dune.

He looked once more at the vast sea of

tents below. Then he slid down the sand to his own little camp. Everyone rushed to him.

"Eric!" cried Keeah. "You gave us such a scare! What happened to you?"

He told them everything.

"The monster's name is Gryndal. The Ninns are building some kind of tower for him. I didn't really understand that part. But the biggest news is that Sparr is gone. At least for now."

Keeah's eyes glimmered. "So it is true. . . ."

"I don't believe it," said Khan with a snarl. "I will never believe it. I can almost smell him."

Neal chuckled. "Unless it's the smell of whatever Eric has in that bag. What is it?"

Eric burst into laughter. "Looks like a Ninn specialty — meatballs!"

Even Khan managed a grin. "But come," he said. "We're wasting time. It's not safe to stay here. Already the scent is growing faint. The monster — and my treasure — are this way!"

Five

Voice of Thunder

The small band trekked through the night.

When morning came they found themselves before a high wall of sand-colored stone.

"Do we stop here?" asked Julie.

Khan shook his head. "No. Gryndal came this way. I'm certain of it."

Keeah scanned the rock. "There is a pass over there," she said, pointing to a break in the rocks. "We can follow it through to the other side."

The kids headed into the narrow pass. Steep jagged walls rose up on either side. They moved through quietly and in single file.

"This is the perfect place for a sneak attack," Eric said. "Everyone be on guard."

The sounds of their footsteps echoed off the rocks. Every whisper seemed like a shout.

Suddenly, a voice boomed down from above. "Stop where you are!"

Everyone froze.

Thwomp! A dark, slithering shape leaped down from the rocks and planted itself in the path before them.

The creature was seven feet tall. It had scaly green skin, thick arms and legs, and a long thorny tail. Horns grew on its head.

Its gnarled face had three angry eyes glowing red.

And its mouth sparked and sizzled with fire.

"It's him!" Eric cried. "The dream monster!"

"And the treasure monster!" Khan added.

"But where is his pig nose?" Neal whispered.

"I am Gryndal," the creature shouted. "King of the elves!" His voice boomed as loud and as deep as thunder.

"Elves?" said Neal. "But where are the rosy cheeks? The twinkling eyes? The cute little hat? That's what elves are supposed to look like."

"Give up your treasure or we shall fight you!" Gryndal roared. "Come, my elves!"

A bunch of other creatures jumped from the rocks. But they weren't like Gryndal at all.

There were six of them. They were three feet tall and wore long orange cloaks. Their faces were hidden by huge hoods. Each had a sack over its shoulder and a fistful of long shiny palm leaves. They waved them menacingly.

But they didn't seem very scary.

"Behold my elves! Ruthless and terrible they are!" Gryndal thundered. "Kindly give them all your valuables and no one will be hurt!"

Keeah snorted at that. "We will not! In fact, we have come to take our treasure back!"

"Oh, want to play tough, do you?" Gryndal boomed. "Then take this!"

Blampf! He shot a blast of fire at the kids. Luckily, Keeah sent a bolt of blue lightning in front of the fire. *Ka-whoom!* The fire vanished.

"That won't stop us!" Keeah said. "Attack!"

In a flash, Khan's tough little arms swung into action, but two hooded elves jumped him and began swatting him with their palm leaves.

They grabbed for his canteen, but Khan tossed it high. Eric caught it and tucked it into his belt.

Neal dashed to help Khan, pulling one elf back by his long cloak. "Eat sand, dune boy!" he said.

Then he grabbed at the second elf and managed to pull off his sack before the elf wriggled away. Neal slung the sack over his own shoulder and helped Khan to his feet.

"I got some treasure back!" said Neal.

"Now let's get the thieves, too!" Khan said.

Another elf swatted at Julie, then lunged at Eric, snatching Khan's canteen from his belt.

"Shiny treasure!" the elf squeaked.

"It's a water bottle!" Eric shouted.

"It's shiny!" the elf cried. "Gryndal wants it!"

He pinched Eric's ears and jumped away, dragging his long orange cloak behind him.

"Looks like they bought the wrong size uniform at the bad-guy shop!" Julie said, jumping to her feet. "I'd say they take . . . an extra small!"

Blampf! Gryndal's next fire blast forced Keeah back against the stones. "Give me that harp," he boomed. "Or be a toasted wizard!"

"Oh, you couldn't play it!" Keeah said. "It's not for creepy lizards like you!"

Gryndal stepped back and took a deep breath. Flames sparked from his toothy mouth.

"Back off, chili-breath!" Julie cried. She leaped at Gryndal. Then something heavy hit the ground.

Clank! Julie looked back. The monster was staring at the ground next to her.

There, lying in the dust, was his tail.

It was thrashing this way and that in the sand.

"Whoa!" cried Julie. "I am tougher than I thought! Score one for the kids!"

Suddenly — *poomf! Poomf!*

Loud blasting noises echoed into the pass. The ground thundered. The air grew smoky.

"Someone is coming," cried Gryndal.

He quickly grabbed his tail and leaped clumsily back onto the rocks. "Follow me, elves. Back to the tower."

Instantly, his troops scurried back into the rocks, yipping and yapping.

Poomf! Another puff of gray smoke shot up from the end of the pass.

"What is that?" Neal asked.

"I don't know," said Keeah. "But it saved us!"

Clippity-bang! Rrrrr-ping! Poof-poof!

A strange vehicle rolled between the high rocks and down the path to them.

It looked a little like an old-fashioned car.

And a parade float.

And a steamboat on wagon wheels.

Choof! With a final blast of smoke, the thing jerked to a stop in front of them. A small hatch opened and out popped a strange little man.

He had fuzzy green hair sticking up in little wisps over his long ears. His fingers were delicate. His eyes were thoughtful. He wore a neat brown suit and silver spectacles on his nose.

"Come on up!" he called down in a cheery voice. "My name is Friddle! Sorry to scare you, but I sensed you were in trouble!"

The friends looked at one another. Then they climbed up to the hatch.

"Thanks!" said Eric. "You came just in time."

"Indeed!" said Friddle. "But we must hurry to get there before nightfall."

"Get there?" said Julie as they all took seats inside the strange car's cabin. "Get *where?*"

"Why, to the tower, of course!" said the little man. "The tower of the elf king!"

The kids stared at one another.

"But won't Gryndal be there?" asked Neal.

"Yes," the man replied. "And all of your treasure, too!"

Six

The Story on the Stones

Choof! Choof! Friddle pulled back on the control lever and a great puff of smoke burst from the stack behind them. The whole wagon shook.

"Forward we go!" cried Friddle gleefully. In no time the vehicle was bouncing over the dunes, spraying sand behind it.

"I'm Keeah," said the princess. She introduced everyone. "Why were you in the pass, Friddle?"

The little man grinned. "I've been following Gryndal. Ever since he appeared out of nowhere nearly a moon ago."

Eric glanced at Keeah. "The same time Sparr disappeared."

"Gryndal and his elves robbed my workshop," Friddle added. "I invent things, you know."

Neal laughed. "I love your motorized cart."

"Thank you!" the man said. He opened a slit in front of the cabin. Warm air rushed in.

"I've made quite a study of elves," he went on. "They like to live in the ground. There are twenty-seven varieties, and most of them are quite harmless. But whoever heard of a seven-foot-tall elf with scaly skin and a tail like a swamp lizard?"

Neal raised his hand. "I never did!"

"Ah, so perhaps he is not really a swamp lizard," said Friddle. "One wonders. . . ."

"Well, whatever he is," said Eric, "he's not just stealing jewels, but water bottles, too."

Julie laughed. "Which reminds me, Neal. What's in the sack you managed to steal back?"

"Yes!" said Khan. "Is my crown in there?"

Neal pulled open the sack he had taken from one of the elves. He looked into it.

He slumped his shoulders. "Oh, man!"

"What is it?" Eric stuck his hand into the sack and pulled out a shiny metal object.

Khan sighed. "A spoon?"

"Not just *a* spoon," said Eric. "*Lots* of them!"

Neal tried to grin. "To eat our meatballs with?"

Puff! Chug! Hisss! The cart bounced along, slipping into the dips between the dunes and roaring up out of them again.

Suddenly, there was another sound.

Pling! Thrum! Blong!

"Yes?" said Friddle.

"Sorry," said Keeah. "It's this harp. Sometimes it plays all by itself. I think it's broken."

"Oh, really?" said Friddle. He pushed his spectacles up on his nose and squinted first at the harp, then at the princess. "May I take a look?"

Keeah nodded.

Friddle's long, slender fingers took the harp. A strange smile crept across his face as he studied it. Finally, he set it on his lap and sighed.

"I remember when I made this —"

Keeah nearly fell off her little seat. "You? You made the harp? Then you must be —"

"The Maker?" Friddle quaked with sudden laughter. "Oh, that silly name! Yes, I suppose I deserve it. I make all sorts of things. But then . . . you must be Kee-Kee?"

Keeah beamed. "My mother called me that! She's Queen Relna!"

Friddle laughed brightly. "I'm sorry I didn't recognize you. It was years ago. You've grown into a fine princess!"

"Thank you," said Keeah.

"But the harp, poor thing, has seen better days," said the Maker. "The story stones are all painted over."

"Story stones?" Julie said. "What are they?"

Friddle pulled back one of the levers. The wagon chugged along by itself.

"Magical gems," he said, turning to the children. "They show the story of a person's life. I set twelve blank ones in the queen's harp. We must restore them to their original beauty. And see what story they tell us!"

Friddle took a bottle off a shelf in the cart, opened it, and daubed a cloth with its liquid. It smelled like raspberries, Eric thought.

"What are the harp's powers?" asked Keeah.

Friddle made a low whistling sound as he wiped the harp with the cloth. "That depends on who uses it and how. It can fly, of course, and talk. . . ."

"Talk?" said Keeah.

"Why yes," said Friddle. "When it plinged just now, it called my name. You just have to learn to listen. Ah, there!"

The harp suddenly sparkled with a rainbow of colored stones.

"See here?" he said, pointing to the first stone. "This shows the castle where your mother was born. And here is the cottage your father built for her —"

"That's where I found the harp!" Keeah said.

"Yes, yes," Friddle murmured. "This dark one shows Sparr's fortress, where something terrible happened."

"She was cursed there," Keeah said softly.

"And here . . . hmmm." He stopped.

"What is it?" asked Khan, leaning over.

"A white falcon," Friddle said.

Keeah peered closely at the stone. "That's what my mother became when she was cursed."

"Next to it is a blue dragon," Friddle said. "And next to that is . . . a . . ."

"What?" asked Eric, craning his neck for a better look. "I can't see."

Friddle held the harp up to the light. "It's a ruby. It shows . . . a . . . red . . . tiger."

Keeah gasped. "A red tiger! That must be what she is now!"

The Maker sighed. "But look. Two

stones are missing. When you find them, you will know the next shapes your mother will take!"

As Eric watched her, Keeah began to smile even as her eyes blinked back tears.

"A red tiger," she whispered. "I'll search all of Droon to find her."

Friddle smiled at her. "I daresay you will."

He pushed and pulled the buttons and levers on the control panel. "And . . . there it is!"

Eric squinted through the cabin's opening at a dark shape twisting up from the red dunes.

A giant tower.

"Wow, that's one big tower," Eric said. His knees felt weak just looking at it.

Khan squinted at it. "Is that ugly tower where my treasure is?"

Friddle nodded. "I'm afraid so."

The tower *was* ugly. The outer walls were made of large slabs of metal. And all the way to the top were Ninns — hundreds of them — hammering the slabs sloppily together.

"Don't tell me we're going in there," Neal mumbled softly.

Julie nodded. "We're going in there."

"I asked you not to tell me that!" Neal moaned.

The cart gathered speed as the tower loomed ever closer. Eric and Keeah peered through the slit in front.

"Um . . . just a suggestion," said Eric, "but shouldn't we slow down?"

"Why?" asked Friddle as the cart sped faster.

"Because . . . we're going to crash!" Neal cried.

"Ever hear of crashing a party?" Friddle said. "Gryndal certainly won't invite us in, so hold on to your seats. We're — going — in! Khan, good chap, press that button, would you?"

The Lumpy king pushed a red button on the panel. *Flink-flink!* Two large metal horns popped out of the front of the cart.

They looked like bull's horns.

"What are those for?" Julie asked.

"You'll see!" said Friddle.

The wagon raced over the dunes. Faster and faster and faster it sped, until —

"Holy crow!" Eric yelled. "Hold on!"

Crunch! The horns on the cart pierced straight through the outer wall of the tower!

Seven

Ninns with Hammers

Plink! A small door popped open in the front of the wagon. Stale air poured into the cabin.

"I think we're inside," Friddle whispered.

"And still alive!" said Eric as they crawled through the nose of the cart and into the tower.

Friddle remained behind. "I'll draw the Ninns' attention away from you. You'll be safe to search for your treasure. Good luck, my new friends!"

Keeah slung her harp firmly over her shoulder and shook Friddle's small hand. "Thank you for helping us. And thank you for making my harp even more precious to me. We'll see you again soon. That's a promise!"

"I hope to be of service, Princess Kee-Kee!" Friddle pulled his wagon away and turned it. Instantly, a troop of Ninns jumped down from the tower and gave chase as the wagon sped away.

"Quickly now, children," said Khan firmly. "Before we are discovered."

Thwam! Clonk! Thwam! Clonk!

The sounds of iron banging on iron echoed inside the tower. Dozens of red-faced Ninns were gathered around a blazing fire in the center.

"I know the Ninn lady gave you meatballs, Eric," whispered Julie. "But these guys look pretty mean."

Eric nodded. "Yeah. Plus they're working for a very bad dude. We can't forget that."

Some Ninns took giant pieces of iron from the fire and banged them into slabs using huge double-headed hammers.

When the slabs were cool, some other Ninns dragged the pieces up a long, circular stairway.

The kids looked up. The black walls continued up as far as they could see. The stairway circled the inside wall all the way to the top.

"The Ninns haven't seen us yet," said Keeah. "Let's get as far as we can before they do."

"That plan gets my vote," said Neal. "Ninns with hammers are not my favorite thing."

Julie looked around. "First rule of towers: The bad guy always lives at the tippy-top."

"Second rule," said Khan. "That's where he keeps his loot. Now, come on. I can almost smell my crown."

Eric gulped as Julie and Khan jumped into the lead. They slid onto the stairway and climbed up quietly. Neal and Keeah were next, then Eric.

The higher they climbed, the more wobbly the stairs seemed to become.

"I have a question," Eric whispered to Keeah. "Why is an elf king building a tower? Friddle told us that elves like to live in the ground."

Keeah shook her head. "I don't know. But I think we'll find out when we get to the top."

The top. Right. Eric knew they were going there, but he didn't like wobbly stairs. Especially because at every complete turn of the tower, there was an opening to the outside. He could see the ground getting farther and farther away.

"Slow and steady," Eric said. "No sudden movements."

Then the stairs began to shake.

Neal turned. "The Ninns are coming! Look!"

Six Ninns were dragging a slab of iron up the stairs. They hadn't spotted the kids yet, but they were getting closer.

"We can't go down," said Julie. "The Ninns will see us."

Khan looked toward the top. "The Ninns will bring that slab all the way up. We can't hide there, either."

Keeah bit her lip and looked around. Finally, she looked down at the stairs themselves. "We can't be on the stairs when the

Ninns come by. So there's only one thing to do."

"Jump?" asked Eric. "Please don't say that."

Neal laughed. "No, dude. I think what Keeah means is . . . we need to hide *under* the stairs."

"Under?" said Eric. "But how?"

"Everyone, take hold of my harp," Keeah said, holding it out. They did.

"Harp, under the stairs!" she said.

Then the harp — with all five of them clinging tightly to it — floated out beyond the stairs and quickly ducked beneath them.

The children dangled in the shadows.

Stomp! Stomp! The Ninns were getting closer.

"Oh, I don't like this," said Eric. "Not at all."

The Ninns tramped heavily overhead, scraping and dragging the iron slab upward. They pulled the slab through an arched opening and began to hammer it into place.

Clonk! Clang! Boom!

After what seemed like hours, the Ninns finally trudged back down the stairs to the bottom.

The harp quickly floated the kids back up.

"Um, that was fun," Eric murmured. "Not."

Julie pointed across the open tower to the stairs on the far side. "The steps end at a door. It must lead to Gryndal's hideout."

They took the last few turns together.

"My treasure is near," said Khan.

Keeah put her finger to her lips and pushed open the door. The room inside was bare.

The treasure was not there.

But something else was.

Gryndal. King of the elves.

His ugly, scaly back was to them.

His tail, which appeared to have grown back, was swishing across the floor.

Gryndal stood in the center of the room, gazing out a small round window.

As the kids slid in, Neal's bag of spoons touched the narrow doorway. The bag made the slightest of sounds.

Clink.

It was enough.

Gryndal whirled around. "What!" he shrieked. "You scared me!"

Eric blinked. "We scared . . . *you?*"

Eight

King of the Hog Elves

Gryndal tried to blast them with a breath of fire. But — *pooof!* — the force of the blast knocked him backward. He toppled to the floor.

Clonk! His leg fell off. Then one of his arms went flying. His tail crumpled and skittered across the room.

Gryndal tried to get up, but something gave out a loud snapping noise. He toppled again. That made his head — the head with three red eyes and a fire-breathing mouth — fall backward like a helmet off his neck. His chubby pink neck.

Gryndal sighed. "Oh, fumbly-bumbly!"

The kids stared at him.

"Whoa!" Neal gasped. "He's fake!"

"Don't come any closer!" Gryndal snorted.

Khan and Keeah edged over anyway. Neal, Eric, and Julie crept up behind them. They kept staring.

Gryndal was not a monster anymore.

Instead of a scary scaly face, there was a plump pink one. Whiskers stuck out of a thick, flat nose with three nostrils.

His legs and arms were short, and his hair stuck out in wispy patches across his forehead.

He had a curled tail with little bumps all

up and down it. He wore a baggy orange suit.

And he was the size of a turkey.

Khan gasped. "Of the twenty-seven kinds of elves, you must be — a hog elf!"

"Aha!" said Neal. "The pig nose! I knew it!"

Gryndal waddled out of the pile of monster parts. "Very funny, very funny," he snorted.

His voice was snuffly and growly. He wiped his nose on his orange sleeve and looked helplessly up at the kids.

"Oh, let me at him!" Khan growled, but Keeah held him back.

"Why the monster costume?" she asked.

"Ha!" Gryndal snorted. "Do you think the Ninns would obey me? Build a tower for me — a hog elf? Pah! They are scared by glowing eyes and puffs of fire!"

"Uh, so were we," said Julie. "A little."

"A lot," whispered Eric.

"But now," the elf went on, "I no longer need the Ninns. My tower is nearly finished. The treasure is on top. And I shall soon be gone!"

"Gone where?" asked Julie. "Up?"

Gryndal snickered and looked nervously out the window. "Perhaps . . ."

Eric looked out, too. Clouds lay like a fluffy carpet below them. *Below* them.

"Looks like we caught you just in time, then," said Keeah. "We want our treasure."

"Yes!" said Khan. "Give it back right now. My people need it — it belongs to them."

Gryndal looked at them. It seemed as if he was going to speak, then he turned away. "I have a duty to my own people, too. That sorcerer Sparr cursed me and my fellows."

Gryndal paused to look out the window again.

Why does Gryndal keep looking out? Eric wondered. *What's going to happen?*

"It was terrible!" the hog elf went on. "One whole year Sparr kept us cursed in the stone mills of Feshu."

"Sparr is gone," said Julie.

"That's what ended our curse," Gryndal said. "But we found ourselves far from our home of Morka. I need that treasure to fly home."

Keeah frowned. "Fly home? How?"

"The soarwings!" Gryndal said. "Giant birds who live in Morka but circle Droon once a year. They fly above the clouds, only stopping for shiny things. That's why I needed the treasure to get their attention."

Eric glanced around. The room's ceiling stood thirty feet overhead. Above that was the top of the tower. Where the treasure was.

The only way up there was out the window.

They'd have to get up there somehow. Gulp.

Hanging from stairs is one thing, thought Eric. *But climbing up the outside of a tower that's higher than the clouds?*

"I need that treasure!" Gryndal insisted. "Because — look! The soarwings are coming!"

The kids rushed to the window.

Far in the distance were two enormous birds. Their giant, bright-feathered wings flapped slowly as they made their way over the clouds.

It was too much for Khan. He jumped up and down, crying, "Give me my crown!"

"Not till I'm through with it!" the hog elf replied. He put his chubby fingers in his

mouth and puffed. Instead of fire, a sharp whistling noise came out. *Eeeee!*

An instant later, his six fellow elves pounded through the door behind the kids. They swished their palm leaves back and forth.

"I think we're outnumbered," said Neal.

"Come, my elves!" Gryndal announced. "We are going home. And no one shall stop us!"

Suddenly — *blam!* The door burst open again. This time, five Ninn warriors stomped in.

They were red-faced, they were huge, they were mad.

And they weren't wearing dresses!

Nine

The Magic Words

The Ninns looked at Gryndal. Then at the pile of monster parts. Then at Gryndal again.

"You are hog!" one Ninn grunted. "Ugly hog!"

The elf king wiped his nose. "Well, yes. . . ."

"Tower is finished!" said another Ninn.

"Give us treasure now!" grunted a third. "You made promise."

Khan jumped. "You promised *my* treasure to the Ninns?"

Gryndal shuffled to the window. "I had to! I needed my tower built!"

Eric didn't know whether to feel sorry for Gryndal or not. His enemy was Lord Sparr. That put them on the same side. But he stole the Lumpies' treasure, and that was bad.

The Ninns glanced at one another. They grumbled for a while. It seemed like they were deciding what to do next. Then they stopped.

Eric guessed they had made up their minds.

"We get you!" the Ninns shouted.

"Stay away from me!" Gryndal squeaked. "Or I shall roar like . . . like . . . like the red tiger!"

Keeah gasped. She trembled. She screamed, "STOP!"

Everyone did stop. Even the Ninns. They all stared at Keeah. She stepped over to Gryndal.

"Did you say . . . the red tiger?" she asked.

Gryndal slid closer to the window. "The red tiger. Yes, I saw her. They say she was a queen cursed by Sparr. I know where she is."

"She is my mother!" Keeah shouted. "Tell me what you know! Tell me everything!"

The elf king looked out the window. The birds were flying closer. "Well, I would, but you see — I must go. I must go — now!"

In a flash, Gryndal climbed out the window.

"Wait!" Keeah cried. She bolted out after him.

The six hog elves followed her.

"I guess it's our turn," said Julie. "Come on!"

But the Ninns came back to themselves. They blinked and growled and got mad again.

"Get children," they shouted. "They help Gryndal! They are enemies of Lord Sparr!"

The red-faced warriors drew their swords.

"Oh! Big swords!" Khan said. "Very big!"

"Get back, you dudes!" said Neal, stepping accidentally into Eric. The two boys stumbled and hit the floor together.

Clang-a-lang! Splat! Their bags full of meatballs and spoons spilled out next to them.

The Ninns waved their swords.

Eric looked at Neal and grinned. "Are you thinking what I'm thinking?" he asked.

Neal smiled back. "Don't hog the food! Everybody — grab a spoon!"

As the Ninns edged closer, the kids all grabbed spoons. They loaded meatballs onto the spoons. Then they pulled back on the spoons . . . and let go!

Fwing! Splat! Plop! Slurp!

The room was a storm of flying meatballs!

"Eek! Aff! Oop!" The Ninns scattered under the rain of meatballs. They shielded their heads. They crouched low. They ran for cover.

Then the meatballs ran out.

"Uh-oh," Julie mumbled. "Out of ammo."

The Ninns made gargling noises. Eric knew what this meant. The Ninns were laughing.

They started after the kids again.

Then Eric remembered something. It

was what the Ninn woman had said in the tent. He wasn't sure if it would work, but he said it anyway. Loudly.

"Thalak!" he yelled.

The Ninns jerked to a stop. They looked at one another, then at Eric, grumbled, stepped back, then tramped out the door and down the stairs.

Neal stared at Eric. "Dude, that was awesome!" He slapped Eric's hand in a low-five.

"Nice choice of words," said Julie. "What does *thalak* mean?"

Eric shrugged. "We'll find out later. Right now, we need to help Keeah!"

He jumped to the window. He peered out and up. The rough surface of the tower jutted above him. The hog elves were escaping up the side.

He gulped. He didn't want to follow them.

But he had to.

Here goes! he said to himself. Eric pulled himself out the window. He clung to the side and began to climb.

"Slow and steady," he murmured. "No sudden movements."

Then there came the terrifying sounds of iron being ripped apart. The tower shuddered.

"Oh, man!" Eric cried. "Please . . . no!"

"The Ninns are shaking the tower!" Khan said, climbing out the window below Eric.

"They're hopping mad," said Julie. "They're tearing the tower apart!"

Neal scrambled up behind them. "Not even spoons will save us now — we're doomed!"

Ten

A Wizard's Journey

Eric's knees felt weak. His stomach fluttered. But he kept climbing, hand over hand, up the side of the tower.

Then, suddenly, there they were. Two enormous silver birds swooping down from the sky.

The air hummed as the soarwings circled the tower. Sunlight glinted off their feathers in a rainbow of colors.

At last, Eric tugged himself to the tower's top.

Standing before him was a huge mound of shimmering gold and jeweled objects.

Khan's treasure.

Keeah tried to rush to Gryndal, but his elves jumped in the way, swishing their palm leaves.

The tower shuddered again. It began to swing back and forth.

"Come here, soarwings!" Gryndal cried out.

Fwap! Fwap! The giant birds descended to the treasure, landing on the tower. They made cooing and purring sounds as they picked and rummaged through it with their long beaks.

In a flash, Gryndal leaped onto the feathery back of one of the giant birds.

His six fellow elves jumped on after him.

"Where did you see my mother?" Keeah demanded. "Tell me where!"

"Beyond the rocky coast of Mintar, near the Bangledorn Forest," Gryndal shouted. "That is where I was cursed. That is where I saw your mother —"

Fwap! Fwap! Gryndal's bird began to rise from the tower. The second bird rose with it. They both pulled away from the tower and circled it once.

"Take your treasure!" Gryndal said, grinning, as he and his men swung the giant bird around. "Take it all! We need it no longer!"

"We are free!" his elves yipped happily. "We are going home!"

Keeah stood there as the tower groaned and twisted with each swing in the air.

Then, in a single swift move, Keeah unslung her harp. She held it before her. And she spoke.

"Harp! Take me up!"

"Keeah!" Eric yelled over the sound of roaring wings. "What are you doing?"

But the harp followed her command instantly. In a whoosh of air, Keeah rose from the tower and swept toward the second bird.

"Keeah!" Eric yelled. "Come back! It's too dangerous! We'll go with you!"

The princess flew up to the bird and leaped onto its back. She gripped the neck feathers and the bird circled the tower once more.

Julie and Neal finally clambered over the top. Khan rushed to the treasure heap and stopped.

They all looked up.

Keeah's eyes sought out her friends' faces one by one. "We finally have the treasure," she cried. "But now I must go. Gryndal knows more than he is telling. I must find out!"

She turned, smiled bravely at Eric, and waved.

"Keeah!" Eric called. "Wait!"

But she rode the giant bird over the clouds toward the sun.

"Eric, we better get out of here," Julie said. "This tower —"

Crrrrk! A chunk of the tower cracked away and fell to the ground. Another huge piece split off and tumbled down.

The tower began to split.

"Uh-oh," said Neal. "I think we've stayed too long at Gryndal's party!"

Khan found his crown and plunked it on his head. "Yes!" he cried. "My people have their treasure back! Now come. We must hurry!" He began to stuff a sack with his treasure.

"Too bad we didn't think of parachutes!" Neal said, helping Khan stuff his sack. "Did anybody think about how we're going to get down?"

Eric gulped. He looked around. "Um, no . . ."

Suddenly — *fwoosh!* — flames rushed up the side of the tower. A bright blue shape floated by.

"Oh, man! Now what?" Julie cried.

"Jump aboard!" yelled a voice.

Eric peered through the clouds. "Friddle?"

"The one and only!" the little man chirped. He was standing in the basket of a giant hot-air balloon. "Come aboard! The tower is breaking up!"

In a flash, Julie and Neal jumped into the basket. Then Khan swung his giant bag of treasure aboard and leaped in himself.

"Whooooa!" Eric took a running jump just as the tower wobbled again. He had barely reached the basket when the tower swung one last time.

But this time, it didn't swing back.

The Ninns cheered as the tower of the elf king crashed to the duncs below. *Kawhoom!*

A moment later, all was quiet.

As the balloon floated gently lower, Eric felt sad and happy at the same time. Keeah was following her dream. With every mile, she was getting closer. But weren't they also losing a friend?

"I wish we could help her," he said.

The Maker turned to him. "And with all our hearts, we shall!" His eyes twinkled as he spoke.

"We'll help her with all the magic Droon can muster," Khan said.

"And inventions," said Friddle happily.

"And teamwork," said Julie.

The two soarwings were now only tiny dots on the horizon. The purple dawn turned golden.

"Keeah's dream calls her," Friddle said. "Yours will call you back here soon. And you will see her again. Your lives are bound to hers. That, I can tell."

Eric looked deeply into the strange little man's eyes. He liked what he saw there.

He liked what Friddle had said, too.

It sounded good. It sounded right.

"The stairs," said Khan. "I see them."

The staircase shimmered brightly atop a high dune. Friddle landed the balloon nearby. Everyone got out.

Khan, with his crown perched firmly on his head, was his cheery old self again. Over his back he slung his enormous sack of treasure.

"Things will be happy again in Lumpland," he said to the children. "Thank you for your help."

"Wait a second," said Neal. "We never did learn what *thalak* means."

Eric turned to Friddle. "I said it to the Ninns and they went away. What does it mean?"

The small man scratched his chin, then roared with laughter. "Roughly, it means — 'I'll pinch your cheeks if you don't go away!' Yes, Eric, I am sure you confused those poor Ninns!"

With that, Eric and his friends raced up the stairs. At the top, they watched the giant birds rise higher and higher into the brightening sky.

Neal flicked on the light.

Whoosh! The floor appeared. Droon was gone.

For now.

"That was one awesome adventure,"

said Julie. "It seems strange that Keeah is just . . . gone."

"We'll find her," said Eric firmly.

"You better believe it," said Neal. Then he added, "So . . . anyone for chili dogs?"

Eric looked at his friends. He couldn't help but smile. "Gotta eat, I guess. To keep in shape for our next adventure!"

Julie started for the basement stairs. "How about . . . last one in the pool is a . . ."

"Hog elf!" Neal yelled. "Snort, snort!"

Laughing together, the three friends charged up the stairs and outside to join the party.

ABOUT THE AUTHOR

Tony Abbott is the author of more than three dozen funny novels for young readers, including the popular *Danger Guys* books and *The Weird Zone* series. Since childhood he has been drawn to stories that challenge the imagination, and, like Eric, Julie, and Neal, he often dreamed of finding doors that open to other worlds. Now that he is older — though not quite as old as Galen Longbeard — he believes he may have found some of those doors. They are called books. Tony Abbott was born in Ohio and now lives with his wife and two daughters in Connecticut.